# The Mulberry Bird

## Story of an Adoption

# The Mulberry Bird

## Story of an Adoption

### by Anne Braff Brodzinsky
### Illustrated by Diana L. Stanley

**PERSPECTIVES PRESS**
Indianapolis, Indiana

THE MULBERRY BIRD has been written with some consideration for the natural habits of birds. However, it is a fantasy, and therefore it is not intended to represent the lives of real birds in any consistent way.

Perspectives Press
P.O. Box 90318
Indianapolis, Indiana 46290-0318

Manufactured in the United States of America.
ISBN 0-9609504-5-1

**Library of Congress Cataloging-in-Publication Data**

Brodzinsky, Anne Braff, 1940–
   The mulberry bird.

   Summary: In the face of insurmountable problems, a young bird mother finds the strength to make an adoption plan for her much loved baby, giving him a stable home and two loving parents.
   [1. Adoption--Fiction. 2. Birds--Fiction]
I. Stanley, Diana L., ill.  II. Title.
PZ7.B78616Mu  1986   [Fic]      86-2460
ISBN 0-9609504-5-1

For my daughter Shoshi

This is the story of a mother bird who lived in a mulberry tree long ago. Although small and young, she was a strong little bird. Her short body feathers were greyish yellow; her longer wing feathers were marked with black and white.

In springtime, in the cool hours before sunrise, she loved to fly in great swooping patterns around the mulberry tree. Her special song could be heard through the singing of all the other birds,

"Per-chic-o-ree,
per-chic-o-ree"

As the spring days grew longer, her body grew heavier, and she knew that it was time to prepare for a baby bird.

She built her nest of twigs and straw on the middle branches of the huge mulberry tree. Inside the nest, which was lined with the soft feathers pulled from her body, she laid one lovely, pale blue egg. She was pleased with the egg and admired it for a moment before lowering her warm breast into the nest to protect it.

When the right number of days had passed, she felt the egg move slightly. As she rose from the nest she heard a scratching sound from inside the egg. Soon the scratching became a tap-tap-tapping, and suddenly the shell cracked!

First the baby bird's beak appeared, then his sweet little feathered body stretched the crack wider and wider, until finally he tumbled out, and the shell fell away completely.

He looked a little surprised at first, but soon began to chirp, hoping that his mother would know that he was hungry.

Mother Bird flew in a circle around the mulberry tree, watching for enemies and looking for food. She noticed that some of the other mothers had father birds to help them. Her baby's father had flown away long before she built her nest and laid her pale blue egg. She knew then that she would have to take care of her baby alone.

She brought only the fattest beetles and the juiciest berries to feed him. She screeched and flapped her wings furiously whenever unfriendly birds came too close to the nest.

One morning, perched on her lookout branch, Mother Bird sensed danger. It was not night-time, but the sky suddenly grew dark. The wind blew in angry gusts against her feathers. Quickly she flew back to the nest to prepare for a storm.

Carefully she spread her wings over the nest and covered her wonderful baby. Deep in her throat she warbled, "Per-chic-o-ree, per-chic-o-ree" so that he would not be afraid.

The storm was like others she had known. The wind blew hard. The rain came pouring down. The branches holding the nest swayed back and forth. Usually birds can protect their nests and babies in storms. Usually after the storm everything is all right again.

But this time was different.

High in the mulberry tree was a dead branch with no leaves or berries. In the wind the branch broke away from the tree. As it fell, it caught on the edge of the nest and pulled away a piece of the carefully woven straw.

The baby bird was crouched in the corner of the nest that was torn away. When that piece of the nest fell, he fell, too. Fluttering his baby wings that were not strong enough for flying and chirping loudly, he disappeared quickly through the wet leaves. As the rain poured down around her, Mother Bird flew to the ground to look for him.

There were many broken branches and whirling wet leaves under the tree, but before long she heard a soft crying sound, and there, next to the tree trunk, was the little bird, trying to stand on his tiny legs. Mother Bird fed him some beetles and berries and tried to shelter him from the driving rain.

When the storm ended, Mother Bird had many problems. She wanted most of all to bring the baby back to his warm nest, but it would be many weeks before he could fly to the high branches where it rested. She knew she had to build a new nest for him, but she did not know how to build one on the ground. Each time she gathered the sticks and straw together, trying to make a nest, small gusts of wind or the baby's flapping wings would scatter them in all directions. When she left to hunt for food, she could not watch for the larger birds and forest animals who were a danger to the baby bird.

20

Mother Bird was afraid. She was younger than the other mother birds, and this was the first time she had had a baby to care for. In the evenings after the baby bird was asleep, she tried to think of ways to solve her problems. In the mornings she flew about frantically trying to build a nest on the ground, looking for food, and calling out warnings to enemies. She worked all day, every day, and later and later into the nights.

Many days and nights went by, but the problems did not go away. Again and again she tried to fix the nest, but it was not strong enough to hold the growing baby bird. She tried to bring enough food to him and to keep him warm, but he was always hungry and crying. Mother Bird was very sad. She did not think that she was taking good care of her baby. She did not think that she could keep him safe and happy.

Tired and worried, she went to see the wise owl, who, it was said, could solve problems that were too hard to solve alone. Mother Bird told him about the storm and how hard she was trying to make a nest strong enough to hold the baby who had fallen. She told him that the little bird on the ground was cold and hungry.

Owl said that he knew a way to solve her problem, but it would mean that she would have to say goodbye to her baby bird.

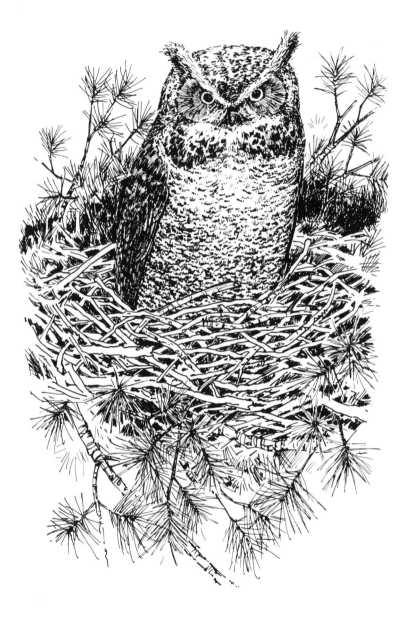

Mother Bird looked at the owl. She did not like what he said. She did not want to say goodbye. Quietly, though, she turned toward him as he began his story.

"Ever since the world began," said the owl, "there have been some mothers who could not take care of their babies. When this happens, sometimes other birds want to help."

He told her that far away on a lovely beach, two fine birds had built a large and wonderful nest in the grass. They were ready to begin their family, and Owl had promised he would try to bring them a baby bird to love.

"I will hold your little bird in my wings and fly with him to the beach. I will place him carefully in their nest and they will adopt him," said Owl. "They will make a safe home for him and care for him forever. They will become the baby's mother and father."

Mother Bird said "No!" She did not want to let her baby go. Silently she flew home alone.

She continued to try to protect and feed the little bird. She circled the mulberry tree screeching and flapping her wings when un-friendly birds came too close. She fed him fat beetles and sweet berries whenever he was hungry. She worked alone, without stopping, hoping for a better answer than the one that Owl had given her.

28

Just as she was starting to feel a little more hopeful, there was another storm. This storm was worse than the first one. Mother Bird huddled over the baby bird as the fierce wind tore at her feathers and the cold rain poured down through the mulberry tree and soaked her body. When the storm finally stopped, she wearily flew off to look for food.

When she returned, the baby was gone. She searched for a long time among the fallen leaves and broken twigs. She looked in the tall grass and even underneath the thorny branches of a nearby rose bush. Finally she found him. He was muddy and shaking with cold. He could not eat the food she had brought.

Mother Bird stood quietly for a few minutes looking at her baby bird. Then she said softly, "I will go and bring back Owl."

Owl looked at the baby bird. He looked at Mother Bird. His face was serious, but he spoke in a kind voice.

"This baby needs a warm nest," he said. "He needs protection from danger. He needs mother and father wings over him in storms."

Mother Bird knew that Owl was right. She had tried to solve her problems, but she could not. Carefully, she helped the tired wet baby into the folds of Owl's warm wings.

Baby Bird was too young to remember all that had happened. But Mother Bird was not. She would always remember.

"All grown-ups have hard problems," she thought. "Saying goodbye to my baby is one of mine."

Flying to her lookout branch, she watched Owl and Baby Bird disappear into the clear sky. "How safe he will be," she thought, "and warm and dry."

Then, taking a deep breath for courage, she flew high above the mulberry tree, higher than she had ever gone before, and, swooping widely in her favorite patterns, she sang... "Per-chic-o-ree, per-chic-o-ree," to say goodbye.

36

All that day and all that night and for another day and another night Owl flew steadily on. On the morning of the third day Owl reached his destination– a lovely sandy beach on the coast. The sun warmed Owl and Baby Bird as they flew closer to the grassy dunes.

Far below on the beach two birds were waiting for Owl. Together they had built a strong nest in the grass. They had waited for a long time. Each morning they had stretched their necks toward the sky and watched for his wonderful wings. Each day they had added more of their softest feathers to the inside of the nest.

Finally, the day had come. High above the waves, they spotted Owl.

He had kept his promise. He had found a baby who needed a home. He had found a baby whose mother had tried, but could not take care of him.

Now they would be the baby's mother and father. The baby would be theirs forever.

They could not wait until Owl reached the beach, so together they flew up over the waves to meet him.

The three big birds flew together for a while. It was a beautiful day. In celebration they dipped and soared— in toward the dunes, out over the surf, and down again. The sun warmed them as they flew. Baby Bird peeked out of Owl's feathers and looked at his new life.

That little bird who had been born in the mulberry tree grew up happily on the beach. His parents told him about his birthmother and the story of the storms and the broken nest. They also told him how hard she had tried to build a new nest and to give him the things that he needed. He learned about Owl and their long journey together. He learned that coming to live with his new family was called being adopted.

Every so often he thought about the mulberry tree. He tried to imagine what it would be like to fly high above it, then swoop down and land in its branches. He wondered what it would be like to live there.

Most of the time when he thought about being adopted, he felt okay. Sometimes, though, he felt sad. He thought about his birthmother. He wondered what color her feathers were and if she ever missed him.

His parents helped him through the sad times. They knew it was hard for him to understand why he had been adopted. They knew that trying to figure it out was something he had to do.

They taught him new songs and took him to his favorite places in the dunes. He learned to love the call of the sea birds, to catch the brightest silver minnows in the foam, and to build a strong and secret nest of grass and down.

While he was young, his father and mother protected him from enemies. As he grew older, they taught him to avoid danger and to solve problems by himself. In winter the family flew with the other birds to warmer places. When spring came, they returned to their beach to build new nests.

He loved the rhythm of their lives together, and, as the years went by, he grew stronger and more sure of himself. Being adopted, he decided, was having two families– one far away but not forgotten, and one that greeted him each morning, surrounding him with the flutter of their warm feathered bodies and the noisy chorus of their singing.

## ABOUT THE AUTHOR

Anne Braff Brodzinsky was born in Providence, Rhode Island and grew up in New England and the midwest. Interested in adoption from the time she was a child, she became an adoptive parent in 1971. A registered nurse who has worked primarily in psychiatric settings, she has also been involved in research and clinical work focused on children's understanding of and adjustment to adoption.

During her interviews with children who had been adopted, she became aware of their intense curiosity about the reasons for their relinquishment. The Mulberry Bird, Mrs. Brodzinsky's first book, was written to help children begin to construct their own answers to these difficult questions.

The author is currently a Ph.D. candidate in counseling psychology at New York University. She lives in South Orange, New Jersey with her husband and children.

## LET US INTRODUCE OURSELVES . . .

**Perspectives Press** is a narrowly focused publishing company. The materials we produce or distribute all speak to issues related to infertility or to adoption. Our purpose is to promote understanding of these issues and to educate and sensitize those personally experiencing these life situations, professionals who work in infertility and adoption, and the public at large. Perspectives Press titles are never duplicative. We seek out and publish materials that are currently unavailable through traditional sources.

Our authors have special credentials: they are people whose personal and professional lives provide an interwoven pattern for what they write. If **you** are writing about infertility or adoption, we invite you to contact us with a query letter so that we can determine whether your materials fit into our publishing scheme.

### Perspectives Press
P.O. Box 90318
Indianapolis, Indiana 46290-0318

## Books Available from Perspectives Press

*Perspectives on a Grafted Tree*

*An Adoptor's Advocate*

*Understanding: A Guide to Impaired Fertility for Family and Friends*

*Our Baby: A Birth and Adoption Story*

*Our Child: Preparation for Parenting in Adoption*

*Everything You Ever Wanted to Know about Planning an Adoption Special Event*